Emma's Freckles

For Ryan, Imogen and Isaac, my inspiration, always. - S.W.

For all the little freckle faces ... never be afraid to shine a little brighter. - L.M. x

Little Pink Dog Books,
PO Box 2039, Armidale, New South Wales 2350, Australia.
www.LittlePinkDogBooks.com

First published 2023

Printed in Singapore by Craft Print Holding Pte Ltd.

ISBN: 978-0-6489641-6-2 (hardback)

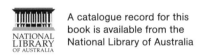
A catalogue record for this book is available from the National Library of Australia

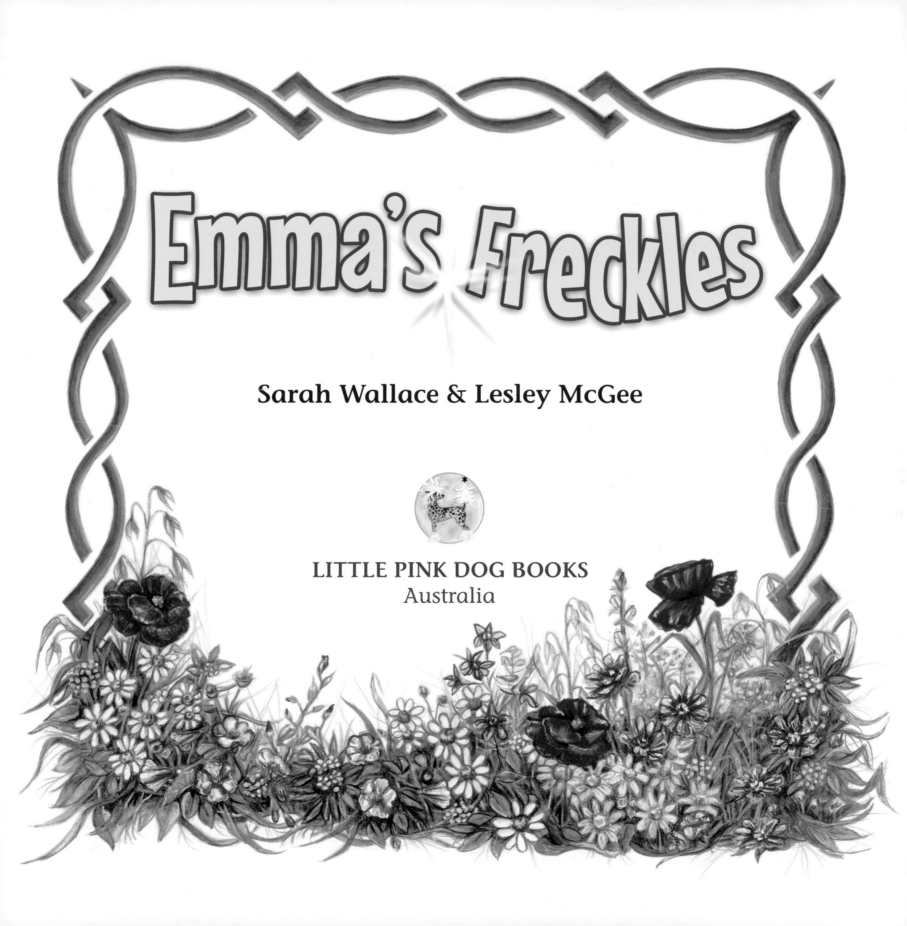

Emma's Freckles

Sarah Wallace & Lesley McGee

LITTLE PINK DOG BOOKS

Australia

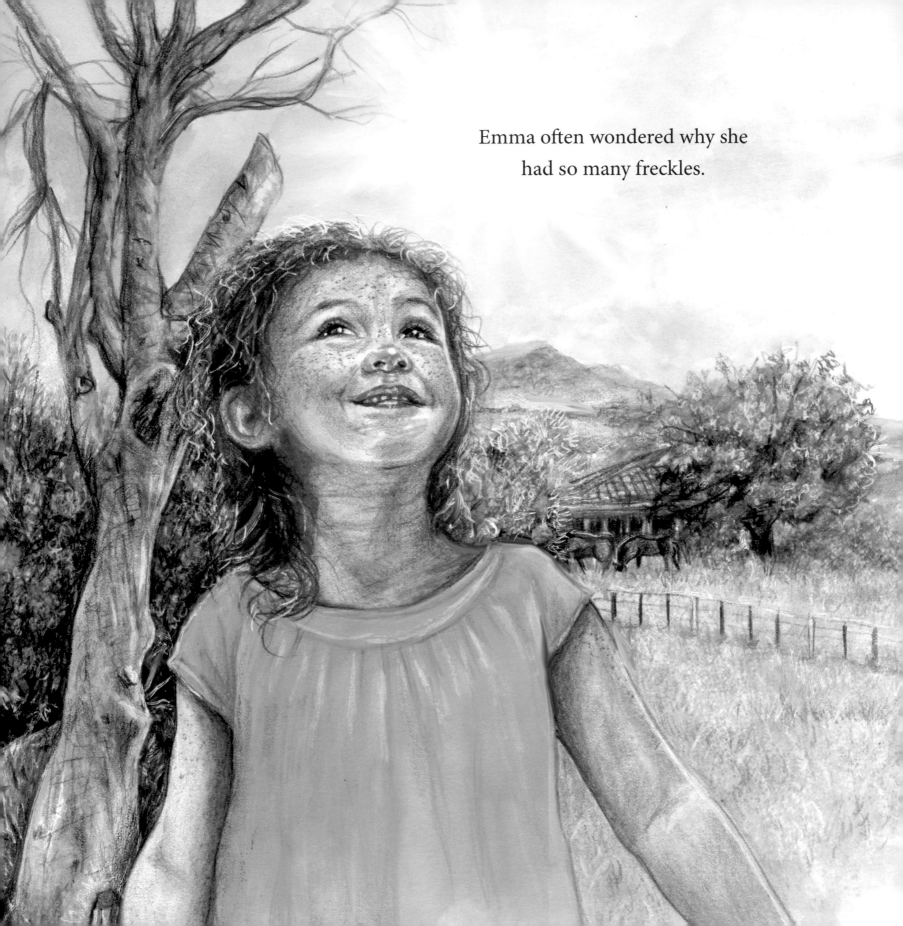

Emma often wondered why she
had so many freckles.

'They look funny,' said Sam.

'You have THOUSANDS of them,' said Milla.

'They're just from the sun,'
said Emma's friend Janey.

That night Emma couldn't sleep.
She pulled back her curtains and looked up at the sky's expanse of glittering diamonds.
She was always enchanted by the night sky.

She picked out the brightest star in the sky, closed her eyes
and wished with all her might her freckles would disappear.

When Grandma came in to check on her, Emma asked,
'Why do I have so many freckles?'

'Oh, don't you know?' said Grandma.
'Let me tell you a story …'

'My people came from an island at the edge of the ocean. It's a beautiful place, with hills reaching to the horizon and rivers that have run for thousands of years.

It is filled with nature's quiet places, where the wind carries messages across the countryside and gentle bird song calls to the hilltops.

The ocean sings songs of wonder, and when the sun
sparkles down, the whole island shimmers.'

'It sounds wonderful,' whispered Emma,
imagining herself climbing ancient trees and exploring wide valleys.

'It is,' said Grandma, 'There is a mist that dances off the ocean and sprinkles dewdrops across the hills and fields.
At night the mist rises to the clouds, like a blanket softly covering the island while it sleeps.'

Emma closed her eyes and could almost feel the cool mist gently brush her arms.
'But can you still see the stars?' she asked.

'It can be hard to see the stars through the mist,' answered Grandma, 'So the ancient gods became worried that people would forget their beauty and wisdom.'

'But how could you forget stars?' asked Emma.

'Well, you always know they're there,' said Grandma.
'But if you don't see them, you can forget how the distant constellations
and galaxies tell stories, and speak to you from faraway places.
They show us our ancestors and our connection to the island.'

'So, the stars are more than just twinkling lights?' asked Emma.

'Yes,' said Grandma, 'the stars help us understand what binds us together.
The gods of the island wanted to make sure people wouldn't forget, so they sprinkled
special dust over the people that covered them in freckles, which they called 'little stars'.

The little stars on people's faces are maps of the stars.'

Emma's eyes widened.
'My freckles show the stars?'

'More than that,' said Grandma, 'They connect us all.
When all the freckled people come together, they form a map of the whole universe.'

It was the most magical thing Emma had ever heard.
'My freckles show my place in the universe,' she proudly whispered,
as she closed her eyes and drifted off to sleep.

The next day, Emma shared her
special story with Janey.

'Wow, I wish I had freckles like you,' said Janey.

When they saw Sam and Milla,
Janey called out
'Emma's freckles are
really important!'

'Yes!' called Emma,
'My freckles make me more
special than you'll ever know!'

She walked away grinning, with Janey by her side.

Milla and Sam looked puzzled.

That night, Emma smiled as she gazed out her window at the glimmering stars above.

'I wonder where the Emma constellation is.'